UNILATERAL

Chris Katsaropoulos

WATERFRONT DIGITAL PRESS

WATERFRONT DIGITAL PRESS
Published by Waterfront Digital Press
2055 Oxford Avenue
Cardiff, California, 92007, U.S.A.
Copyright © Chris Katsaropoulos, 2014

Cover art and design for *Unilateral* by Brit Godish.
Cover images courtesy of Shutterstock.

Printed in the United States of America

10 9 8 7 6 5 4 3 2 1

Praise for *Antiphony*:

"What I found most engaging about *Antiphony* are the questions it raises . . . The story is fascinating, and the writing is powerful and poetic."

—Joseph Yurt, *Seattle Post Intelligencer*

"*Antiphony* is a book so eloquent and brilliant that it requires time—that precious entity few seem to have saved for exploration of the arts—to explore this obvious treasure. It is related to the great works of literature—James Joyce, T.S. Eliot, Virginia Woolf, Solzhenitsyn, Dante Alighieri, Roberto Bolaño, Tolstoy, Proust, Kazantzakis, Kafka, Melville, and Conrad."

"Katsaropoulos's grasp of physics is astonishing as is his ability to phrase theory in a manner comfortably decipherable. His deep entrenchment in literature and in music blossoms on the pages frequently. His grasp of the manifold variations of human relationships breathes of psychology breeding with philosophy. But most of all it is the serene beauty of his writing that mesmerizes and results in starting the book again once finished that proves this is a man of letters who has an enormous gift and future."

—Grady Harp, Amazon Top 10 Reviewer

"Hold on to your chair or you will be totally transported out of your comfort zone by *Antiphony*. It doesn't matter if you haven't the foggiest idea what String Theory is. . . What does matter is that you will fall down a metaphorical rabbit hole alongside a scientist driven to prove his theory. Katsaropoulos is an emerging fresh literary voice not to be overlooked."

—Rita Kohn, *NUVO Newsweekly*

"*Antiphony* is, in many ways, an awe-inspiring novel. It was, I think, written in awe. Awe of science and reason. Awe of intuition and faith. Awe of the one and the many . . . Katsaropoulos has a way of delving deeply into what seem like small moments and capturing all their nuances and vibrating tension."

"It makes me wonder how he did it."

—Al Riske, *Thoughts with Nowhere Else to Go*, author of *Precarious* and *Sabrina's Window*

"I enjoyed this book a lot. *Antiphony* is super smart but also accessible. It delves deeply into scientific theory as well as philosophy and some psychology but uses layperson language and felt really accessible to me."

"The writing style reminds me of Milan Kundera. I'm a huge fan of Kundera's work... so this is a big compliment. I think Kundera has a really unique voice and style that I never see anywhere and Katsaropoulos has a similar quality that lent some magic to the reading for me. *Antiphony* blends reality and non-reality in a fabulous way."

—Kathryn Vercillo, *Diary of a Smart Chick*

Praise for *Fragile*:

"*Fragile* is a beautifully-written novel . . . the writing is uniquely refreshing. After reading *Fragile*, I found myself feeling very contemplative. Readers will enjoy *Fragile* and will find meaning in it that applies to their own lives . . . Highly recommended."

—Paige Lovitt, *Reader Views*

"Mesmerizing and beautiful, a truly stunning book! Katsaropoulos's first novel sets the bar incredibly high. In what can only be described as a truly unique style, the author takes us from the thoughts of one character directly into the next: an ongoing narrative of a brief portion of these three lives, to a moment of intersection so hauntingly profound and exquisite, it will leave the reader astounded and deeply moved."

"With a debut such as this, I see a wonderfully promising future for this author. A story and characters you will never forget, with a message as old and true as time itself. I have already read this twice, and marveled at it even more the second reading. I cannot recommend this book highly enough! A true classic for the ages."

—Lauri Coats, *ReviewTheBook.com*

"There is an element of higher meaning in this story that makes it fascinating to finish and to contemplate the experience of reading it. For lovers of experimental literature, this book is tasty."

— Grady Harp, Amazon Top 10 Reviewer

Also by Chris Katsaropoulos:

Novels

Fragile
Antiphony
Entrevoir

Poetry

Complex Knowing

UNILATERAL

"STAY HOME," AMEL'S mother says, pouring warm milk into a coffee cup, there being no coffee available to drink. "The cease fire ends today." Mother hands Amel the cup, and as Amel takes it from her, she hears a faint cracking sound, so faint she isn't sure where it's coming from. The surface of the milk is starting to form a thin light-brown skin, where the milk has cooled, and Amel has to take a spoon and skim the skin off the top before she can have a sip, wishing all the while that the milk were really coffee, and that her mother would stop talking to her about fear.

"They have been bombing—over by the university… a lot." Sometimes, when her mother gets excited, her sentences become broken, chopped up by pauses in odd places, stops and starts.

"They're bombing everywhere," Amel states casually, as if this would make her mother feel better.

"It's true," her father says, unexpectedly. He is such a gentle and quiet man, it's often surprising to hear him speak. "We can't stop living." He glances towards the blade of morning sun piercing the gap between the shutters of the front window, looking for a signal that may indicate whether what he has said is true.

"You go," her mother says, pausing, "to work. Bashaar goes to—work. Amel doesn't need to go to school."

How fearful they have made us. These are the words that are forming in Amel's mouth, but she doesn't allow herself to say them. She is calculating the shortest distance from the table that dominates this one small living room of their apartment and the front door. The less she says now, the better. Her father has already stood up for her, in his own meek way, and Bashaar is bound to start spouting some nonsense about repression and uprising and rebellion any minute now. No matter how annoying Bashaar can be, at least he is a free spirit. He seems determined not to follow in Father's footsteps, seems desperate for any means of getting out of Gaza. The low droning music he plays, the clothes he wears, the way he gels his hair in imitation of French rap singers or Spanish soccer stars, all of it seems to be in direct contradiction of everything Mother and Father have provided for him.

"Be back for lunch," Bashaar says. "The more buildings they blow up, the more work for me." Bashaar has been invigorated by the latest conflict—no one has bothered to call it a war yet. He claims it will mean more work and more money, in the long run, but Amel knows the real reason he is excited by it, a secret she has sworn never to tell their parents.

Amel skims another thin layer of skin off the milk and brings the cup to her mouth, blowing across the surface to cool it. Again, she hears a very faint tinkling sound, as of ceramic cracking. Before taking a sip, she raises the cup higher, to eye level, to see where this quiet little sound is coming from.

"Just stay away from the—hospitals," Mother says. "The schools, they are… bombing them."

"I go where the work is," Bashaar says, defiant. "We build wherever things have been knocked down." He can afford to be rude to her, he brings home most of the money for food. Ever since he got the job applying plaster of Paris moldings in construction projects, he has been acting like the real man of the household. Father goes down to the harbor to work; most days he comes back empty-handed.

Now Amel can see it, holding the cup close—a tiny jagged white crack at the joint where the handle meets the rim of the cup. This minute imperfection, a fault-line in the ceramic, emits a very soft creaking sound as she carefully places the cup back on its saucer without having taken a sip. Perhaps the heat of the milk made it crack, or could it be merely a flaw in the design of the cup, the way it was made? Hands free, she swipes at the face of her phone to check the time: 7:49. If she doesn't leave in the next two minutes, she'll be late. She shoves her textbooks into her back-pack, slings it over her shoulder and makes a move for the door. The less said, the better, not even goodbye.

It's only two steps from the table to the front door. Their apartment is tiny, cramped, like everything else in Gaza, crushed to fit the most compact area available. This living room, crammed with furniture: the table where they all eat, chat, do homework, listen to the radio, watch TV, the bureau where the dishes and all their other belongings are stored, plus the narrow divan beneath the front window where Bashaar sleeps. There is one other room, the lone bedroom, which contains two twin beds, one for her parents, the other for her, and also the cooktop where meals are prepared, a refrigerator no taller than her waist, and the cabinet where clothes are hung and dry goods are stored. The outhouse is in the courtyard behind the building—complete with a plastic cup to pour water down the toilet and chase away the flies. If she wants to take a bath, maybe twice a week, her mother will heat enough water on the cooktop to fill a metal tub she can use in a secluded corner of the courtyard, shielded from the prying eyes of the boys on the upstairs floors of the building by the climbing green vines of a grape arbor. That's all there is to it, her home. She doesn't mind being here, but she has to get away; she can't stay here forever.

With her hand on the door handle, her mother calls her back.

"If you must go… take the casserole—to the bakery." The pauses between Mother's words make them sound like lyrics, words to a song she will never sing. "We'll have it for… lunch."

Mother scurries into the other room, her back hunched with worry, and returns with a large round metal pan filled with potatoes slathered in olive oil. Every second or third day Mother plans a big meal like this, too large to cook on the burner in the back room. Amel accepts the pan from her with both hands and nods, more to indicate that she needs help with the door than to say goodbye.

Father is quick to react, slides by them and pulls the door open for Amel, pleased to have something to do. The only one who has the guts to say anything more is Bashaar.

"They'll be bombing us before noon."

"Don't say that!" Mother practically shouts at him—she has a superstitious belief that any word or statement or command that comes out of one's mouth is destined to become reality.

"They'll break the cease fire before we do, just to show they can."

"When you… talk like that Bashaar—you know it makes me sick!"

Mother is correct, she knows he says things like this just to spite her, to get her worked up; it's one of his newfound channels of power, alongside his status as primary bread-winner. He has discovered and proven through his own teenage obduracy Mother's theory of the power of words. Amel sees that this argument has transferred Mother's attention and fear away from her and towards Bashaar and uses the distraction to slip past her father's outstretched arm holding the door open for her... and she is free.

The simple calculus of four people cohabitating in two tiny rooms has always compelled her to go outside to the streets and alleys and random plazas of their ramshackle neighborhood and roam. Two steps down from the tiny front porch and onto the dusty street, the heat of the August morning is already building—it will be nearly a hundred degrees by afternoon. She can feel her breath stifled by the fabric of her burqa. Her footsteps echo against the walls of the apartment buildings that press in against both sides of the dusty street. There are no gardens or easements here—no patches of green. Everything is concrete, cement, sometimes she feels as if the entire world is fashioned of concrete. Their street is so narrow it doesn't even allow for cars to be parked on it—one lane for an occasional car or truck to pass through, sidewalks on either side and then the canyon walls of two, three and four-story apartment blocks to the right and to the left. It's only a few footsteps to the end of the block where her street intersects with a larger road and the bakery with its inviting glass windows occupies one corner.

Intisar, the shopkeeper, sees her and comes to hold the door open so she can enter.

"Come in, come in." Even as she ushers Amel into the shop, Intisar lets the door close behind her and in nearly the same motion takes the casserole from her. "Let me help you with this."

"Thanks—I'm in a hurry. Late for class."

"You know, the cease fire is ending—we may be closing."

"I'll pick it up on my way home." Amel looks around the shop; it's more than a bakery, it also serves as a kind of convenience store for the neighborhood, selling newspapers, milk and other drinks, candy, cigarettes, and it has a phone, which some people use to make calls via land line if they don't have a cell phone. Sometimes Father comes here to make long distance calls to Uncle Emad in Cairo. And, in one corner, the squat freezer where various kinds of ice cream bars are stored. Since she was a young girl, one of her favorite things to do was come here on a Sunday afternoon with Father, open the silver lid of the freezer, reach down without looking through the cloud of cold air that rises like smoke, and pull out whichever ice cream bar her hand happened to select. Intisar has known Amel since she was a girl, and has taken casseroles like this from her countless times—she will bake the dish in one of the huge ovens at the back of the store alongside the day's pastries and bread.

"We may close early," Intisar says, repeating her warning.

"I know, the cease fire. I'll be back by noon!" With this, she gives Intisar a little wave and hustles out of the store. Everyone is in a hurry, the traffic on the big road seems more urgent than usual, everyone trying to accomplish a week's work in a day. She doesn't usually like to rush around, usually enjoys the three mile walk across the city to class, but this morning she picks up the rhythm of the people alongside her, moving along with their urgency to get everything done as soon as they can. She hurries by the sandwich stand, Marwan the owner already carving slivers of meat from the skewer into waiting slices of bread. The smell of sizzling beef makes her hungry now that she has skipped her cup of milk, arguing with Mother. The jumble and noise of the shops and the people brushing past make her feel happy—this is the world she is accustomed to, crowded, noisy, flooded with sensations. In the past two days everything has returned to its normal chaos, and she has almost gotten used to it again. The tailor's little hole in the wall is open, as is the first of many car repair shops she will pass, its storefront a garage door wide open and displaying a scene of leisurely manual labor framed in the intense brazen light of an electric arc lamp hanging from a wire. A dark man in a white sleeveless t-shirt swings a sledge hammer down from high over his head and pounds, pounds, pounds on a piece of rusting sheet metal. Is he repairing it or destroying it?

Amel rushes past the man's swinging hammer blows. There's a place next door that sells used books and CDs, worn second-hand clothes and copies of old magazines from Europe and America. Sometimes Amel stops in and browses the books—the shopkeeper is kind, lets her read, though she hasn't bought anything in more than a year. Alongside the bookshop is a kind of factory. Amel thinks of it as a place where all sorts of things are built, though she isn't quite sure what product is made here. She sees men going in and out, and some women too—and large crates being loaded onto trucks at all hours of the day. Somehow, they produce something here that people will want to buy. It always amazes her, how all the people crammed into her corner of the city get by on so little. She tries not to think about it too much, but where does all the money come from, how does everyone have enough to eat? Only a few of the men she knows have real jobs—most of them sit around at the café on the square and play backgammon or cards, sipping tiny cups of coffee and arguing about politics. At least Father goes to the waterfront and tries to find work every day.

Two more streets to pass and she will be on the main road into town. A hunched older woman scoots over to avoid a telephone pole in the middle of the sidewalk and knocks into Amel's shoulder, brushing her aside in that way the old ladies often have, as if they have earned the right to be rude by having suffered longer than you.

"Hey," Amel says, more by way of surprise than anger.

The old lady turns her head and glares at her for a moment. Amel stops, and it seems as if something more might be said. The old woman's eyes narrow through the gap in her burqa, then turn away, and she is gone, hustling on to whatever it is she is hurrying towards.

The jolt of the old woman's shoulder reminds Amel that she's running late—perhaps she will take the shortcut. There is a route she can take that cuts the angle towards the center of town, more direct than the main road, but it goes through neighborhoods with narrow streets and fewer people—some streets where she has seen gangs of boys standing around, watching her pass by with their eyes lifting the veil from her face, streets where she doesn't usually go. She hears her mother again and Intisar warning her, fear in their voices. Better hurry, come home soon. So she crosses the road and enters the side street, shadows of the apartment buildings still eclipsing the morning sun.

Most streets in the city bend or curve, crossing each other at odd angles, at one time long ago they were dirt paths the sheepherders followed, trails animals used to take from one watering hole to another. This makes the walk more pleasant. The view towards the end of this street is balked by a bank of apartment buildings where the road turns to the north, angling directly to the center of town. This street is quieter than the main road, she can hear her own footsteps echo off the concrete walls that line either side, and she can proceed more quickly here, fewer people to avoid, fewer distractions from storefront windows. Her mind returns to the argument with Mother this morning, which was a variation of the same argument they have had dozens of times before, with a different rationale to motivate her mother's harangue—why do you have to go to school, Amel? Stay home with me and tend to the household, the chores, this is women's work, let the men go off to earn the money. Why do you have to learn about languages of other countries, France, England, America? What good will they do you here? Even Amel has come to question what she is trying to accomplish, what has driven her to trudge across the city twice a day to study verb conjugations and computer word processing when it is likely she will never leave this fenced-in patch of land on the edge of the sea, never have the chance to visit those faraway places.

At the bend in the road, she can see up ahead in the next block a gathering of men standing around what looks to be a construction site. As a precaution, she crosses the street to walk down the other side, increases the pace of her footsteps. This is what she hoped to avoid and why she doesn't like coming this way—the isolation of this street, the prying eyes of men. She tries to distract herself from the thoughts of men apprising her form by thinking of Bashaar working at a place like this, imagining Bashaar here at this site watching out for her, condemning any of the men who might say something vulgar, or stare at her figure swaying in the robes she wears as she moves past. Bashaar comes home from work soaked in sweat—he is allowed to bathe every single day. But she tries not to think about the work he does too much, for he carries a secret with him even as she carries the secret form of her body with her shielded from view by the bulk of her robes.

As she draws closer, she can see this is not a construction site. There are many unfinished buildings in the city, apartment blocks with two or three stories completed, people already living in the building, with the next floor partially complete, exposed wires and pipes and bent re-bar steel jutting out, waiting for more money to come so the work can continue. This is not like that—this is a pile of rubble, a dozen men standing by in jeans and t-shirts, young boys in replica soccer jerseys, most of them covering their mouths and noses with their hands. Two of the men are coming up from the hole in the ground dragging a wheelbarrow full of gray dirt and plaster, struggling to bring it to the level of the street. When they do bring it up, two of the boys help them tip the barrow over and dump the contents into a pile. The latest cease fire has been going for two days, so this is not a new hole. The boys and men don't even notice her as she moves closer, they are intent on their work. And now she knows why they have their palms to their faces, covering their noses and mouths—now that she is close enough to see that this is a hole in the ground where an apartment building once stood, she is overcome by the stench of rotting flesh. She puts her hand to her mouth, to the cloth of the azure blue burqa that covers her face but is not enough to keep that wall of smell out. The taste of it makes her want to spit, though she knows she cannot do that here. She moves faster—how she wishes she had not come this way. She can see more, things she doesn't want to see but cannot take her eyes from: at the foot of the pile of rubble, a small dog covered in dust and dirt, a stain of dried blood on the street where it has been lain. And this too—another pair of men emerging from the hole, one of them, an older man, bald, in a short-sleeved dress shirt spattered with blood, carrying the limp body of a young boy, the boy's small form lifeless, his arms and legs splayed out, eyes closed, mouth open, his head appears deformed, there is something terribly wrong with it. Amel wants to take her eyes away from the boy's head, but she cannot. There it is, emblazoned within the clutches of the older man's despair—his head slashed open, black hair torn away and only blood and bone and pinkish gray substance showing underneath where his perfectly formed head should be, his mouth open, as if there were still a reason to breathe.

THIS IS SUCH an open place, the wind whips across the vast expanse of the airfield, bouncing the sun around, slapping against the planes. He loves to come out here in the morning and see it, his plane, his. It waits for him in the morning sun, gleaming dull silver, wings tipped with blue. He ducks under the fuel tank and pauses near the landing gear, inspecting the metal struts and checking to see that each of the tiny tires is properly inflated—the worst thing he can imagine is flying a flawless mission only to have a tire blow on landing and rip the plane apart. Everything looks perfect— everything ready to go. He loves to see the underside of the plane, the intricate structure and form of it modulating in a series of smooth sweeps and curves, like the tender expanse of a woman's hip. The wind brushes against his hair, dips under the airfoil. From the shadow of the wing, he can see across the staging area to the broad open field where the main runway waits, fifteen thousand feet of empty pavement, waiting for him to perform. He tilts his head from under the wing and looks up at the sky—unlimited ceiling, blue as far as he can see, a couple of cotton puff clouds sliding across the western horizon for decoration. Perfect day for flying. Back under the belly of the plane, his plane—his name is inscribed under the canopy, RA'ANAN COHEN COMMANDING OFFICER—he places his hand against its swollen underside, the gently rounded center of it, where a hidden cargo resides, his passengers as it were. He will deliver them safely to their destination, always has and always will.

He will take them where they need to go. He rubs the seam in the sheet metal, lined with rivets, the slot that will slip open when he delivers his babies, pats it twice for good luck, precious cargo that must get to where it needs to go.

BOREDOM IS BETTER than fear. At least now that she has made it to class, a little late, Amel can try to take her mind off that boy they were pulling out of the rubble. The professor gave her a look but didn't say anything when Amel came in six minutes late—she was already lecturing on how to set up tab spacing within the page layout of a document in the word processing software they have to learn as part of this computer class. There are so many required courses Amel has to take before she can devote herself fully to her major, she spends most of her time on boring subjects such as computer applications, college algebra, and microeconomics. After a few more minutes describing the lesson and pages in the textbook they will be covering today, the professor allows them to log in to their computers and start the lab. The sheer boredom of this makes Amel have to focus, step by step to complete the assignment... open the document, then type some text, then select the paragraph, then click on the page layout menu blah blah blah. After a few minutes of this, she begins to feel sleepy, her eyelids begin to droop. She shakes her head to wake up—no coffee again this morning—and looks around at the other girls in the lab, no boys allowed, heads down in the computer screens, all shrouded in their burqas. Amel has only one class this semester she can really look forward to—Introductory French Conversation and Grammar, where she has a chance to speak French with the professor and other students, soaks in every word and phrase she can remember. Next semester she will be

able to take two language classes—
Introductory English Conversation as well as
Grammar and Intermediate French. She's a
little nervous about it. Some of the other girls
who are further along have told her that English is much harder than French.

By the time she has finished slogging
through most of the assignment, the professor
comes around and looks over her shoulder,
appraising her work.

"Okay, well done—ten minute break." She
dismisses them with a languid wave of her
arm, shawled in a black robe. No one is in a
hurry here. Though the professor said ten
minutes, they will all linger in the courtyard,
stretch it well past that, wander back to the lab
when they please. The courtyard is an open
area surrounded by the high concrete walls of
the technical institute on all four sides, plenty
of shade from the midday sun, several wooden
benches and a couple of sickly date palms no

higher than an elephant's shoulder bending up from the dirt floor. Amel shares a bench with two of the girls she knows from the class—one of them is also in economics with her and they sometimes discuss the impenetrable graphs and equations they have to memorize, checking each other to see whether they have understood the reading before the next quiz.

Loila nods her hooded head towards the opposite end of the courtyard. "Your boy-friend is back today..." She trails off the last syllable in a flirting rising accent. Amel turns to look. Yes, he is there in his tight soccer jersey, along with two others, the boy who has been staring at her during these breaks from the computer lab every Tuesday morning. There is no question of saying anything to him, she could not bring herself to do that... or maybe she should. She has been hoping that he would come over to the bench they have staked out as the girls' side of the courtyard and talk with them, but so far the only thing he does is stare, and it is clear to Amel and the other girls that he is staring at her. They even tell her so.

"Amel, he thinks you are hot." Loila lets the last word trail off in a sexy way, so flirtatious and lewd that it is all Amel can do to keep from laughing. But she cannot let herself laugh now, because the boy, whose name she doesn't even know, might think she is laughing at him, at his eyes bearing down on her.

All the girls tell her she is pretty, but how can anyone really know in these layers of robes they make her wear. There is a mirror that can sit propped up on the table in the parlor at home, which father and Bashaar use for shaving, but there is rarely a moment when she can be alone and look at herself without her robes, without her underclothes. Mother or Father, or Bashaar could walk in on her at any moment. These girls at the college are her mirror, and the eyes of the men who follow her down the street, and now the eyes of this boy in his tight red and blue striped jersey. It is so tightly fitted across his chest, she can see every contour of the muscles—not one of those silly body-builders—but strong with broad shoulders that make her have a fluttery feeling inside her.

"He's not looking at me," Amel retorts. "He wants you."

"No way!" Loila laughs, breaking the spell. "I've seen the way he watches you—go over and talk to him, what's the harm? The worst he can do is ignore you."

"Or call me a whore."

Where did that come from? Amel just blurted it out, an automatic response such as one of those computer programs will make when a certain command has been entered into the machine. Yes, now she remembers— something Mother said the other day, about a girl she saw talking with Haitham, the son of

Intisar the shopkeeper, at the corner store, calling her a whore, as they turned and headed back home. Mother has a plan in mind for Amel and Haitham—has been trying to arrange their marriage for years, ever since Amel was thirteen, of course the payoff being all the money and prestige of joining with the family who owns the corner store and bakery, a big step up from day laborers and fishermen. Amel has never quite recovered from the day two years ago when Mother told her to bathe and dress in her finest blue burqa because they were having guests visit that evening. Mother cleaned the house all afternoon, turned the radio to the station that only plays howling traditional music, set out plates of sweets and cups of coffee and tea, and even got Bashaar to sit still for a few moments while they awaited their guests. When Intisar and the boy Haitham arrived—Intisar widowed since the Six Day War and Haitham's father, her second husband, also killed in one of the lesser conflicts—no one knew what to say to break the awkward silence after Mother "presented" Amel to them, as if she were selling them the duvet from the day bed. Father finally spoke up and said there would be benefits on both sides—Amel is a beautiful young girl, fertile, and would provide Intisar and Haitham with plenty of strong sons to run the store for years to come, ensuring the legacy of vigorous commerce and wealth would continue to grow. And of course the Jileb family would be honored to join with Intisar's family and, in a sense, make it whole again, with a sanctified and holy marriage in Islam. After which Intisar whispered something in Haitham's ear and the boy's face turned pale. This had been a complete surprise to the boy, though Intisar must have known this could be coming. Finally, Intisar politely rose and set her cup of tea on the table and said they appreciated the offer and would carefully consider it, which at the time to Amel seemed just as humiliating as someone calling her a whore.

Nothing ever happened after that. Apparently Amel's charms were not enough of a dowry to Intisar, or an enticement to Haitham, to make the marriage happen. And enough time has passed that Amel doesn't even feel awkward any more when she goes to the store—it's like it never happened.

"I think he likes *me*," Narmeen says, the third member of their little clique. "I'll go over and talk to him, ask him for a cigarette. If you ask a guy for a cigarette, it's like you're telling him you're loose, you don't care what you do to your body."

"Yeah, go ahead," Loila says, laughing. "He's just lit one."

The concrete walls surrounding the courtyard rise up on all sides, encasing them in this shadowy column of air, shielded from the sun.

The burnt orange of the boy's cigarette glows in the semi-darkness as he takes a drag, the acrid scent of its smoke drifting across the enclosed space.

Narmeen shies away from Loila's challenge. "I can't be bothered, he can come to me if he wants me." She changes the topic abruptly. "Did you see what happened at the zoo the other day?"

This comes out of nowhere. Amel says, "I didn't even know there was a zoo."

"Yes, in the cultural park, on the north end of the city. I go by there sometimes with my brothers, just to get out of the house. They built it a few years ago, with a soccer stadium, some rides and a few buildings that are supposed to be some kind of museum. A tourist attraction, I guess, though we don't have any tourists."

"I heard about that," Loila says, duly distracted. "I heard they have lions."

"Yes, the lions are starving, along with all the other animals. We went over there the other day, just for something to do, and it was awful. The animals are all dirty and sick, underfed, starving in these filthy cages. And then the worst thing is they had been hit by one of the airstrikes. There's a huge hole in the ground, God only knows what cages and animals may have been there, but the other animals all look scared to death. There was a peacock huddled up against some kind of little harmless rodent and a bloated crocodile on a rock near a dried up pond. My God, it was awful."

Amel tries to envision what these animals look like, most of them she has only seen in pictures in books. And the image of the hole Narmeen describes brings her mind back to the body of the boy being carried out of the rubble.

"Why would they bomb the animals in the zoo?"

Narmeen always has an answer, a theory about everything. "I think the resistance put some rocket launchers there, in the park, amongst the cages. They'll do anything to hide them. I saw one in the alley behind our house the other day, and one of the neighbor women came out and started yelling at the men to move it, take it away from our homes."

Amel doesn't want to tell them what she saw this morning, doesn't feel like describing it.

"They're not targeting, they're slaughtering," Loila says. "We're no different than those animals in cages—we're inside a giant fence, we have nowhere to go."

"The worst thing," Narmeen says, "is the people who don't get killed and have no homes. Last week we had to have my uncle's family come to stay with us, all seven of them crowded into our tiny apartment on the fourth floor. Who knows when they will be able to go back to their place? I have to sleep with my cousins now, three other girls and one creepy boy who likes to watch me undress for bed. They eat all the food, I have to be first up to get anything for breakfast in the morning."

"I had the same thing happen," Amel says, "in the last intifada. My uncle was killed and my aunt and cousins stayed with us nearly a year, as well as my crazy hunched-over grandma. My cousin had to sleep in the same bed with me, at least she was a girl…" Amel remembers how the girl, Liyana, would curl up against her in the middle of the night and hold her in her sleep, murmuring about something happening in her dreams, sobbing occasionally, sometimes waking from a nightmare screaming, her body like a little heater in the bed beside her, sweating and shaking. "Eventually, their building was re-built and they left."

"I don't see these people leaving my place any time soon. Where will they go?" Suddenly,

Narmeen, who always seems so sure of herself, lets her voice drop lower. "Loila is right, we're trapped, in a giant cage."

The boy across the way snuffs out his cigarette on the ground by stomping on it, still staring at Amel. His eyes on her now are like two glowing piercing lights, penetrating the shadows. Narmeen's story of the zoo and the relatives crowding around her are constructing a tight, compressed feeling in Amel's chest. Everywhere she turns, someone is watching her, something is blocking her way. Even if she does learn these languages and completes her degree, what opportunities are there for a woman to teach or go to the places where the languages are spoken? She has dreamed of visiting Paris, London, New York—she may as well be learning Swahili for as much good as these languages will do her.

Loila stands and smoothes her dark hair under her burqa, pronouncing her judgment. "There's no way out for us."

Amel doesn't like it when Loila talks like this, even if she feels the same way. She stares at Loila's dark silhouette against the shadow of the opposing wall, feels the presence of the boy's eyes watching her. Amel stands as well and turns; every direction she faces, a concrete wall surrounds her. Every decision she makes is caught within the razor wire of circumstance. She looks up at the rectangle of clear blue sky above her, blue unbroken by any barrier, clear blank nothingness stretching from here to the invisible stars and a thought is given to her, a possibility of truth so clear, she speaks the words softly so that only she can hear them, though she does not know precisely what they mean.

"The only way out is up."

RA'ANAN HATES TO be grounded, hates to be on the ground. The sky is where he longs to be. Since the latest cease fire started three days ago, air command has limited their missions, he hasn't flown in over forty-eight hours, and he can feel the open sky pulling at him, the inverse of gravity, the sensation of being lifted up, which he loves, as his fighter bomber elevates from the runway, it feels less like flying than simply having the earth fall away from him and then, suddenly, he is up, in his natural element, with nothing but deep frozen blue in front of him, a clean and uncluttered vast openness unlimited by any human lack or impotence.

These are the thoughts and images sailing through his head, his best attempt at imagining, though he is lying flat on his back on his bunk in the officers' quarters, staring at the white acoustic tiles in the ceiling only six feet above him.

He has to share a room with another pilot, who is at the moment annoying him by watching a random series of videos on his phone in the midst of playing a mindless computer game. His doing both at the same time makes it even more distracting. Ra'anan closes his eyes and tries to imagine something else, what it will be like once he is out of the IDF and flying wide-body commercial airliners for one of the big carriers, spending hours upon hours each day in the sky, off the ground most of the day on the longest international routes he can manage to fly—transatlantic New York to Paris, Rome to Addis Ababa, London to Hong Kong, twelve or thirteen hours straight through. He doesn't care where he ends up, as long as it's not here. Vered, his fiancée, wants to stay in Tel Aviv, the suburb where her parents live, where he and Vered met and grew up, but he's grown tired of the feeling of being pent up here, and there are only so many places El Al flies, though it would be the easiest airline to jump to after his experience in the military.

The phone his roommate holds in his hands emits a sequence of high-pitched bleating sounds, followed by the creaking echo of a tiny bell, unceasing, tallying up his latest score.

"Narkis, can you turn that thing off?"

Narkis keeps playing, urgently tapping at the screen of the little device to produce more of the high-pitched noises. *Tap-tap-tap-tap-tap.* And then another series of bell sounds, chiming like a slot machine that just hit the jackpot.

"Sorry," Narkis says, finally, laying the thing down beside him. "Had to beat the level."

"I don't care if you play, just maybe turn the volume down. That beeping sound and the bell are pretty goddamn annoying after a while."

"Sorry." Narkis takes up the phone device again and starts tapping it, this time followed by silence.

"Thanks," Ra'anan says, and starts tapping his own phone, to see what's going on outside this tiny room he's trapped in. He checks the news sites first—no attacks from the terrorists in nearly two days, though some Islamic extremists are threatening to behead another American journalist in Iraq if the Americans' bombing raids continue. Perhaps Syria or Iraq will be his next destination. Either one is fine, as long as he can fly. Checks the results of English and Spanish soccer matches—Manchester United continues to struggle.

Reads an opinion piece in the *Jerusalem Post* about the UN's crimes against humanity. Checks his messages—two from his parents and one from Vered, which he opens.

Hey, hope you're okay and doing well. Can't wait to see you again! I've been thinking about us a lot. Dad says we can have the beach house in Bat Yam after we're married. Can't wait to start our life together, hoping it will be sooner rather than later. xxxooo Vered

He taps on the message and starts to type a reply, then pauses. That's Vered, Miss Time Lapse, always looking to the future, always planning how things will be, since he's known her and especially now that they are engaged, she's had this vision of what their lives will be like, has it all mapped out in stages—first we'll do this, then we'll do that, get engaged and then married, Daddy will give us the beach house and it will be close enough to Ben Gurion airport that you can fly with El Al and then we'll have children, two or three, and they'll attend the international school and so on until the kids have graduated university and next thing you know all their lives are nearly finished, dead and gone. It can be a little stifling. So he has been fantasizing lately about living abroad, working for one of the big international carriers, living in one of the major hub cities, Frankfurt or London—maybe Chicago or New York, just to break away from too much planning. And fantasizing maybe also just a bit about not getting married to Vered.

He puts the phone down for a moment and thinks about it—what that would be like. There are lots of other women in the world, and it's a big world for a man who can fly anywhere. But he can't stand the thought of all those plans being shattered, the thought of breaking her heart. Any time his mind starts to wander away from the intricate structure of anticipation Vered has assembled around their lives, he imagines the moment of actually telling her he no longer wants to marry her and the look on her face shames him into remorse for something he hasn't even done.

He picks up the phone again and taps out a note.

Missing you. Haven't been flying much, maybe that's a good thing. We'll be together soon. Stay safe — love R

Sends the note and stares at the acoustic tiles above his head. It's not that he doesn't love Vered, it's just that he doesn't like having his life whittled down to one certain designated path. That is the opposite of flying, the opposite of unlimited ceiling—that's being tied down to a single two-lane highway going nowhere.

"Holy fuck," Narkis says, slapping his open palm down on the bedspread with a loud smack. "I can't believe it."

"What?"

"That sonofabitch, he really is a traitor."

"Who?" Ra'anan says, sitting up. "What're you talking about?"

"God damn it," Narkis says, sitting up too, tossing the phone down on his bed. "My stupid screw up of a brother. He really has lost his mind."

"What happened?"

"He's a refuser. Refuses to enlist, and now he's going to prison for it." Narkis slaps his hand on the bed again, as if the bed has caused this problem. "That sonofabitch, I've heard him talk about this before with his screwed up friends from the coffee houses and the drug addicts he hangs out with—'Oh, we feel occupied too, we're living in an occupied country, occupied by the military.' Well, how about if we just step aside and let those animals come in and chop your heads off, how occupied will you feel then?"

"So, he just refuses to serve?" Ra'anan has heard of such things before, but everyone he knows has served, it's part of life, part of growing up in this country. He never even thought to consider not serving, it was never an option. He always knew he wanted to fly, and the air defense is a very effective way to learn everything he needs to know, using the best equipment ever made. And when there are terrorists blowing up busses and cafés and cinemas your mother or father or sister may be in, you don't think twice about wanting to protect them from those threats.

"Yes—this is his time to enlist, and he refuses to go. So they've thrown him in jail." Narkis looks at his phone again, as if he might find a new message there that will tell him something different.

Ra'anan considers his words carefully, decides to speak. "Maybe he's afraid."

Narkis looks at him and shakes his head. "No... I know my brother. He may be an arrogant idiot, but he's not a coward. He really believes these things he's saying, believes in what he's doing. I've heard him talking about it long before today." Narkis lies back down on the bed and stares at his phone. "I'm just concerned about what will happen to him now. He could be in prison for a long time. Who knows what this could mean for him?"

Ra'anan considers what Narkis has said. He's never had to weigh whether it might take more courage not to fight than to simply do what seems normal and necessary. There has never been any choice—serving in the IDF means protecting everything he's ever had in his life, his family, his home, his country—his future.

Ra'anan has an answer for him. "He needs to be shown what these beasts are capable of—what kinds of atrocities they unleash on their own people. I've seen plenty of videos of Hamas executing Palestinians in the street who were members of another faction—another militant group. Anyone who opposes them. They don't care who they kill, as long as it serves their ultimate goal of destroying us." Just thinking about it makes him want to go on another mission. "Hasn't he seen these things? Doesn't he know they would rather sacrifice their own children as human shields, than allow Israel to exist?"

"He's seen it. He knows." Narkis shakes his head and then lets it drop, stares at the gray linoleum floor. "Listen. This is something he has told me. He said he would rather be killed or see his family killed than have the blood of another person on his hands."

Ra'anan looks at Narkis and tries to contrive a response to this. It's as if a charcoal shadow has descended from the ceiling onto his head, shrouding his thoughts with a layer of fine black dust. There should be a very clear way of approaching every decision, every act—the instinct for survival should override every other basis for action. He looks at Narkis, and all he can think to say is, "That's insane."

The shroud of black dust from what Narkis has said makes him want to go outside, remove himself from this conversation. He stands and heads for the door, excusing himself with an old standby. "I'm going out for a smoke."

Outside, in the grimy parking lot between the barracks and the security fence, Ra'anan pulls a pack of cigarettes from his hip pocket and lights one, drawing a soothing cloud of tar and nicotine deep into his lungs. He can't make those words Narkis said go away—there is something deeply disturbing about them. Ra'anan's life has always been an unchallenged arc of success, progressing from one accomplishment to the next, in school, in athletics, and now in the service of his country, a steady upward ascent towards a glorious future. The only hint of failure he can recall is not being selected for the highest echelon of his club soccer team—there was a moment that day when he realized what it felt like to not succeed, and he knew he never wanted to have that feeling again. Yet even that experience of failure served him—he turned it around and used it to help him focus on what is most important to him, his decision to become a pilot of the highest skill and service to his country.

So why is it now that the decision of Narkis's brother to fail, to choose withdrawal and shame and perversity, is draped around his own head like a soft black cloth?

Ra'anan paces towards the security fence, twelve feet tall, the outer perimeter of the base, with its double row of razor wire looped across the top as if it were a string of savage Christmas lights. He wants to get rid of this shroud that has been placed by Narkis's words on his head, tries a couple different lines of thought to remove it. Takes a long drag on the cigarette and tries to imagine what his father would think of him pulling a stunt like refusing to serve—he would likely throttle him. His dad is a tough old scoundrel, only a baby when he was brought to Israel to live in a refugee camp shortly after the holocaust, grew up with the nation while earning a modest living from tending a small orange grove at first and then eventually opening his own dry cleaners in the burgeoning suburbs of Jaffa—still a hard worker, never turned down the opportunity to be at the store, which eventually emerged into a small chain of three. Ra'anan knows Israel has always been a special case, a tiny nation carved out of someone else's land—a nation thrown together as a solution and reparation for all the past injustices, a nation of refugees that has created even more refugees. Fighting for their existence is the only way he has ever known, the only way to preserve this slender corner of the world they were given. The idea of telling his father he refused to serve is repugnant to him, a burning sensation of stomach acid rising in the back of his throat.

He tries another line of thinking, lets his mind drift back to the note Vered sent him. Remembers the last time he saw her, at her parents' house on the coast, which could soon be their house, her promise of the house with its underlying enticement for him to set the date of their wedding. They have talked about October, several times, over dinner at restaurants, or long car rides together, but he has not been ready to agree to that. A couple of times he has mentioned spring, June, closer to the end of his enlistment. But something is still holding him back. Perhaps it is Vered's need for control, as evidenced by the lists she is always making: lists of errands she needs to run, lists of clothes she wants to buy, random lists that barely make sense to him, all jotted down in her loose looping handwriting. He has a clear image of scraps of paper at the beach house last month while he was on leave, with two of her lists scrawled on them:

Dad's checking
Screwdrivers
Money

And the other one:

Kitchen stuff
Boxes
Coffee
Nuts
Bedding
Measuring cups & spoons

He's not sure what it all means, but the memory of them is endearing to him, picturing these notes written by her scattered around a house that could someday be theirs together. She would make a very good wife for him, a very good mother for his children. Her face looms large in his imagination, in the middle distance beyond the barbed wire, in that other world outside of the base, a world of freedom and yet also a world hemmed in by borders that constantly need to be defended from enemies whose preeminent desire is to see them perish.

"Vered."

He says her name aloud, trying it out on his tongue, listening to the sound of it. It has an open, welcoming sound to it, open at the beginning, but closed off, shut down at the end. He lightly touches the fence as he turns to complete another lap of pacing, tosses his cigarette through the wire. And as he slowly shuffles towards the barracks, he feels a sudden twinge in his right arm, an electrical surge that envelops it from above his elbow down through his wrist and fingertips, as if a low-level buzz of lightning wrapped itself around him, a strange otherworldly presence. It gives him enough of a shock that he shakes his whole arm, to get rid of it, to knock it away. The sensation is so odd, he turns and looks to see what might have jolted him, what might have grabbed him. It could not have been the fence, it's not electrified. Looks around him on all sides and sees there is nothing there.

AMEL HAS THE nagging sense that there is something she forgot to do. On her way home from class, she takes the main road, avoiding the shortcut and that horrible pile of rubble. Passing through the commercial district with its bustling shops and office workers hurrying home for the midday meal, she allows herself to imagine that she's in another city, Athens perhaps, or Rome—still a Mediterranean place, but far enough away that she can pretend to be another person, a language instructor with her own school, teaching immigrant Arabic children the local language, or English and French. People pay good money to learn another language, to help themselves find work and adjust to the local culture. She can imagine living in a modest home of her own, maybe a flat in a modern apartment building with its own kitchen and bath, walking through the city to and from her school, teaching young children and even adults how to read, write, speak another tongue. And perhaps, eventually, there will be a man for her to love, a young handsome Italian or even an Arab, yes, if she were able to fall in love on her own, without having her mother select him. She pictures this street as her new home, a place that has enjoyed life without air raids for many decades, life without fear. And imagines herself, also, walking down the sidewalk in western clothes, a snug pair of jeans shaping her hips and thighs, a colorful top that shows off the rising curve of her breasts—not every day, no. Most days she would continue to wear the burqa, she is a Muslim and will always be. But she would like to be able to choose how she dresses, choose to be a modern woman sometimes, without fear of being condemned for it. The men can do it, why can't she? Still, in the midst of these wanderings, she has the sense there is something she must do, some task she has forgotten to finish. With her mind in a faraway land, she takes her eyes off the pavement for a moment and stumbles, her simple flat shoes caught up in the hem of her robes.

"Watch where you're going," a hairy middle-aged man with a straggling wisp of a beard glares at her, has to do a nimble kind of dance step to one side to avoid her. She gathers herself enough so that she keeps her balance, does not fall. Slings her backpack over her shoulder again and thinks, where *am* I going?

There is something she needs to do. The thought enters her head to go see her brother. Why, she does not know. But she has always been one to follow an intuition, has always found that when she does so it leads to an adventure she would not have otherwise encountered, some unexpected reward. Feeling steadier now, less distracted, she turns at the next corner and heads towards the district where Bashaar has been working.

No destination is very far in this city. Within a few minutes she has left the taller buildings and their gaudy storefronts and finds herself in a neighborhood rather similar to her own—though it's in the opposite direction of home. Two- and three-story apartment blocks, some of them damaged by the bombing or under repair, boarded up windows in some of the shops, this area seems to have suffered more of the airstrikes, perhaps because it's closer to the border. The streets seem brighter here, emptier, baked by the noonday sun. One of the houses on a jagged angular corner appears to have been converted into a makeshift filling station and garage. Two lonely ancient gas pumps stand idle in front of the door where a man leans against the frame and watches two others wrestling a flat tire from a car. The men doing the work are hunched over, kneeling on the asphalt in a pose similar to prayer, their arms reaching out to grapple with the intransigent rubber. Beyond them, the sidewalk is littered with a display of hand-woven baskets, dull brown reflecting the beams of the sun. A woman squats on a tiny wooden chair with a woven straw seat, does not flinch as Amel goes by, the woman's hands a bundle of fluttering rhythmic energy working the dried reeds into a cross-hatched pattern of form.

Amel has been here once before—last week, when she had to bring Bashaar his evening meal. He had run out of money before the next pay packet and couldn't be let off for dinner. It was later in the day, more shadows, street lamps twinkling in the dusk. Perhaps she has made a wrong turn? Nothing looks too familiar.

She remembers there was a mosque at the main plaza of the district, a beautiful tall mosque, narrow and majestic, its minaret rising above the dingy apartment blocks like an arrow aimed at the moon. Blue tile and golden filigree arching across the entrance, calling to the faithful. In the distance, she can hear the lovely lilting voice of the muezzin, chanting his enticements to the noontime prayer. *God is greatest... I bear witness that there is no deity but God...* The dolorous voice from the loudspeaker in the tapering tip of the minaret echoes across the canyons of the buildings, across the centuries, calling to her. *I bear witness that Muhammad is the Messenger of God...*

She follows the voice, which leads her to him. This, she remembers now, is the way.

As she approaches the plaza, she sees the families of the neighborhood filing towards the mosque, led to their worship. She follows them and heads towards the welcoming arms of the mosque, a ritual she has done thousands of times, as much a part of her life as sleep and meals. Then she remembers, the construction site where Bashaar is working is just across the way, down a diagonal avenue that leads directly to the border wall, only a few hundred meters to the east. She veers off and heads down the avenue, rebuking the glances and stares of those headed to worship. It's okay, she has skipped prayer before, has been called a sinner. She hurries now, against the grain of the worshippers headed the opposite way, they too in a rush to make it to their destination on time. Another block or two and she sees it, the frame of the new building, its gridwork of steel girders and beams only partially sealed with concrete walls, the second story merely a set of rusting columns jutting into the dull leaden blueness of the sky. The front wall of the building is comprised of cinder blocks with an unfinished open doorway where some of the workers are passing through.

Why has she come here? She looks for Bashaar and still doesn't know. She'll know it when she sees him.

One of the men at the doorway holds his hand up to stop her.

"What is it?"

He's young, maybe twenty, but has a look of authority about him, could be one of the men who run the crew.

"I've come to see my brother, Bashaar. Is he here?"

He appraises her, looks her up and down with suspicion. In a place such as this, anyone could be an enemy.

"He's working. What do you want?"

She doesn't know yet, has to make something up. "I have something to tell him, a message from home."

He looks her over again, scrutinizing her as he might a bewildering foreign object. Attacks at a site such as this may come from anyone, another militant movement, a vengeful rival looking to gain the upper hand.

"Okay, you can go, just for a moment." As she passes him, he places his hand on her upper arm, then grips it, holds her in place and squints directly into her eyes. "You tell no one what is happening here."

She can only stare back at him blankly and nod.

Inside the shell of the building several workmen are staring down at a rectangular hole cut into the dirt floor, ringed with litter and scraps of electrical wire. It's hard for her eyes to adjust—the oblong lozenge of glare from the doorway is the only light shining through here. One of the men comes towards her and she blinks to register his face.

"What are you doing here?" It's Bashaar, his voice lowered so the others will not hear.

"I have…" she pauses and considers what it is she wants to say. "Something told me to come here—a feeling I had. Something I have to tell you."

"What happened—have they started bombing already?"

"No, nothing like that…" Now that she's here, there seems to be no reason for her to have come, nothing more to say.

"Well, what is it?" Bashaar glances over his shoulder at the others behind him. "We're about to stop for prayers."

She surveys the scene and thinks about what Bashaar must go through every day to earn the small sums that support their family, a teen-aged boy covered with filth and sweat in the confined space of the tunnel, digging it out with a shovel and his bare hands. Some of the tunnels have collapsed while they're being constructed, killing workers, some of them are being blown up by the Israelis. This is the secret Mother and Father don't know about. Bashaar's construction job is digging tunnels for smuggling contraband and carrying out attacks against the Jews. It's true that the tunnels are necessary, they're the only way to circumvent the blockade and keep supplies coming into the city. But what would Mother think about Bashaar joining up with the resistance? She's convinced that he's helping build new apartment blocks, doing plaster work and heavy lifting.

Seeing Bashaar's face covered in a mask of sweat and dirt, a phrase, a holy verse comes into her head, she hears it within her in the same manner as the muezzin would call it in service. *Exhort them, your task is only to exhort, you cannot compel them to believe.*

"How hard is it to stop a war?" she says, staring at Bashaar. "As hard as it is to stop for prayers."

"What are you taking about?" He glares at her and glances around at the others again, concerned they may have heard her.

"Why are you doing this, Bashaar? Isn't there some other way to make a living?"

"Leave me alone. I've chosen to serve what is just and true. I've chosen to fight for the lives of our people, and for God. The whole world is watching us, and they will see that our cause is just."

Amel observes him, hears in his words the words others have told him, and takes a step back, towards the light of the door. The other boys and young men can sense now some kind of a conflict between them. One of them starts to come near. Again she hears the words inside her, echoing in her heart as they would from the heights of the tallest domes of the mosques. *Exhort them, you cannot compel them to believe.*

"If God is the creator of everyone and every thing," she takes another step back, her form engulfed in the light of the door, "He does not need us to fight his battles for Him."

Now, with his cohort right beside him, Bashaar's voice has become loud, angry. "Get out of here, you pig. We won't stop fighting until every last one is a believer, if it takes us a thousand years."

She stands in the doorway for another moment, her vision of him blurred with tears, hearing in a dim, echoing corner of her consciousness words she cannot be sure whether she has spoken, or whether they are his: "The word of God speaks for itself."

THE CALL CAME when he least expected it. He had been in his bunk again, dozing, trying to shake off that strange feeling that came over him out by the fence of having someone, or some thing, grabbing his arm, when the call to scramble came. It only takes a matter of minutes to gear up and get into his plane. They practice it all the time. And now here he is again, exactly where he always wants to be, fifteen thousand feet up in the cockpit of his Viper cruising just under Mach speed. He knew the terrorists would be the first to attack, couldn't wait for the cease fire to be over, had to get the first word in, launch one of their makeshift rockets at a village in the south, just across the border. No matter how high the walls are, how much razor wire adorns the top, those animals find a way to lash out, with their rockets or their tunnels, any way they can to strike terror into peaceful Israelis trying to live their lives. He scans the cockpit display, checks the primary flight display down and to his left, radar and ground maps, then a quick glance at system display, engine, slat and flap settings, fuel and weapon status all go. Another glance at the heads-up display to check flight information and then a look over each shoulder out the canopy, always shifting his eyes to avoid velocitizing them, always checking and cross checking his displays and the visual environment of the clear blue sky around him. Clear blue sky and unlimited ceiling. Perfect day for flying. He has three other Vipers with him on this run, Narkis to his left and two more on his right wing. They've made a giant circle out over the Mediterranean, to allow themselves time to form up and dive in for target acquisition. The cargo he has in the belly of his plane is a smart bomb that uses satellite signals and GPS navigation to zero in on coordinates already pre-set by the ground crew based on IDF intelligence information. Not like the old days when they had to dive in and use the jet's own momentum and angle of attack to slam the bomb into a target. Intelligence already determines the exact coordinates of a tunnel entrance or rocket nest that needs to be taken out, and he can drop his payload from a lot further away and let the GPS take care of the rest. A lot less dangerous, and a lot less fun than it used to be.

Narkis is in his ear with a few final instructions. "Target acquisition in T-minus two minutes. Begin descent and break formation."

Ahead, Ra'anan can see the coastline spread out before him, a giant tan arc of desert marred only by the hazy white blur of Gaza City hugging the water. Display reads ten miles to target. Narkis and the others have peeled away and spread out, seeking their own targets and making them harder for enemy radar to spot. This is when it gets interesting. He bears the stick down to increase the angle of attack to about 45 degrees, and he's brought his airspeed way down to just under 500 knots, and still slowing.

"SAM lock at 2 o'clock." Narkis again, his voice rigid, no emotion at all. Ra'anan jerks the stick right, then left, rolls the Viper over so the horizon flips to vertical, then the sky is underneath him and the sea is where the sky used to be, above his head. Flying upside down. Shaking off the radar lock of the Surface to Air Missile. Leaves it this way for a few seconds, then jerks the stick left right left again, shimmying the upside down aircraft before rolling back over to its usual ground underneath him orientation. Sees a missile fly by him, not even close, probably shoulder-launched. No way in hell they're going to hit him with one of those.

Ra'anan checks his systems again, particularly the weapons status. All go. Ready for delivery.

Half as a whispered reminder to himself, half for the others to hear, he recites from memory his favorite verse from the Book of Joshua. "And it came to pass, as they fled from Israel, that the Lord cast down great stones from heaven upon them. They were more that died with hailstones than they whom the children of Israel slew with the sword. Then spake Joshua to the Lord, and he said in the sight of Israel, Sun, stand thou still upon Gibeon, and thou, Moon, in the valley of Ajalon."

Narkis again, in his ear, not even acknowledging what Ra'anan has just said.

"Begin target acquisition and firing sequence."

Ra'anan has always used that verse as a means of clearing his head, just before delivering his payload. A reminder to himself of the reasons why he is carrying out his mission, of his sacred duty to defend his homeland and the people who rely on him to do so.

Eases the stick up a bit to level off his angle of attack, airspeed down to 440 knots. Slow, slow and steady now, a few more seconds until he lets loose. Checks the heads-up display, all clear, then over his left shoulder and over his right. Then, straight ahead of him, something strange has appeared, two banks of dark gray cloud, spanning about thirty degrees of the horizon, two walls of gray cloud tinged with white coming together like the gates of a castle wall closing.

No matter. He'll bust straight through it, once he has target acquisition and presses the button, the GPS will take his payload where it is destined to go.

At 440 knots, it only takes a couple of seconds for this bank of clouds to come up on him. There were no reports of weather at the target site prior to take-off, no indications on radar of any turbulence in route. Still, sometimes the proximity of the sea kicks up a cloud bank like this in the afternoon heat. Nothing to worry about.

The clouds are like a giant wall with a gate closing before him. The gap between the two cloud banks is shrinking down to a sliver of blue, lined with the golden white reflection of the western sun. In the next instant, he is upon it, enveloped in the gray wispy fog of the cloud bank and no visual ground sighting of the target.

Doesn't matter—he doesn't need to see what he's hitting. The computer does all the work these days. All he has to do is get near enough and press the right button.

Checks his displays one last time and lets Narkis know he's about to fire. "Target acquisition complete." Reaches over and... hears a voice from somewhere say his name.

Ra'anan

Looks over his right shoulder, where he heard the voice coming from, as if he were in a two-seater and the co-pilot behind him called out to him. Nothing there. But he could have sworn the voice came just over his shoulder, as if someone were hovering right behind him, calling to him in a deep, raspy whisper.

He taps his helmet twice on the right side, to make sure there's nothing wrong with the earphones. Then radios over to Narkis.

"Narkis, did you say something to me?"

Instead of a response, he gets static, and when he glances forward to his heads-up display, he sees the gray wisps of fog surrounding his canopy go dark, then suddenly erupt into a searing burst of white light. His first thought is that he has allowed the plane to drift into a deep stall, disoriented by the cloud bank and the steepness of his angle of attack. Then, an image appears, in the orange afterglow of the white burst in his eyesight—perhaps he has been hit by a SAM? An image dilates within the orange afterglow within his eyesight, image of a bus exploding, image of blood red blood spattered across the whitewashed walls of the bus station, white-gray pavement splattered with crimson violent and bold. Image virulent wounds of children's limbs expounding cruel blundered jealous plunged in fear a Roman soldier directing others to the slaughter thousands upon thousands executed slain and diminished for all the luminaries of heaven wane and descend there jealous in fear. Image in orange vision descent of the descending angle of attack at the Park Hotel seder disguised as a woman suitcase bombing explosive suicide detonated the device of the exploding instantly were killed the father along with his daughter the second Intifada claimed responsibility for the massacre angle of attack then spake Joshua to the Lord, and he said in the sight of Israel, Sun, stand thou still upon Gibeon, and thou, Moon, in the valley of Ajalon the martyr brigades blew themselves up and took all the other fathers mothers sons and daughters with them in Qibya an example for everyone maximal killing naked chunks of body parts startled abruptly synonymous spirits fly out and flee their shattered mosques and homes shorn of flesh turned over wives and schoolgirls desecrated for amusement they were more that died with hailstones than they whom the children of Israel slew with the sword. Image this in his vision burst open to see all the litany of iniquities that has burdened this land down through the centuries. One after the other the attacks and counter-attacks massacre the keepers of the temple mount the holy land the

fount of wisdom ghosts run rampant here.
Now he can see what he has become part of,
what his next right action could never defend.
Dynamite and mortar barrage mined the roads
so no one could flee in the Cave of the Patri-
archs the Kach wreaked of blood havoc over-
lapping Purim Ramadan in the litany of the iniquities no one can escape the blame neither
side avoids reprisal, in the litany of iniquities,
no one is guiltless and only the innocent suf-
fer, dead and buried in the mutual lust for
vengeance self-righteous slaughter. One infant
decapitated, another at Khan Yunis and Rafah
camps of tents of refugees fedayeen tied to a
Jeep and pulled limb from limb stench of
cordite against the caravanserai wall lines of
dripping draining blood must flow. In his fear-
riddled vision images one after the other occur
and re-occur and disappear into the rolls of
dead and injured raped and wounded the ter-
rorist came to the entrance and I shot him

twice in the head demoniac on the ground against the smoke noteworthy from ample dispatch and through that oath the sun and the moon complete their courses. Exhort them, you cannot compel them to believe. And now he can see the face of a girl with a blue burqa wrapping her head, eyes silver gray and lips soft as the skin of ripe cherries looking to the sky to the swift solid sound of a jet passing by and releasing its cargo traveling hatched and salvaged to the ground where a hole in a half-completed building boys crouching and trembling, he sees it hit her and release its cloud of smoke and burnt orange black fire stretched across the plain mid-day buildings in due bondage her body blown apart her face set aflame her carcass strewn across the road he sees. The word of God speaks for itself. And he hears now these words in his earphones, crackling with static, in that voice which was too low to be a man's voice, too brazen to be a voice of this earth:

She is more precious than rubies, and all the things thou canst desire are not to be compared unto her. Length of days is in her right hand; and in her left hand riches and honour. Her ways are ways of pleasantness, and all her paths are peace. She is a tree of life to them that lay hold upon her; and happy is every one that retaineth her. So shall they be life unto thy soul, and grace unto thy neck. Then shalt thou walk in thy way safely, and thy foot shall not stumble. When thou liest down, thou shalt not be afraid; yea, thou shalt lie down, and thy sleep shall be sweet.

His eyes open wide, he feels that same sharp tingling of electrical charge from before surge up his right arm, the arm that controls the stick.

He pulls back on the stick and feels the nose of the plane rise up so that he is looking straight up now, at the last remaining hole between those two banks of cloud that have forged themselves together around him, one last hole of blue sky with the tawny gold filigree of the sun shining through. He pulls the Viper up and into a long left roll, out of the cloud bank and away from the target, rolling up and out towards the Mediterranean Sea.

They will all wonder what has happened to him, why he failed to deliver his payload. They will all wonder what happened to Commander Ra'anan Cohen and where he went.

Where will he go?

He figures he has enough range to reach Turkey or Cyprus, perhaps even Greece. He'll have to give them plenty of advance warning, let them know what the hell he is doing, that he's not attacking them and is only seeking asylum as a deserter, a refuser, who refused to drop another bomb and kill another dozen or two dozen persons. What will he tell his father, his mother—Vered? Whatever it was he has just witnessed flashes back to him, slow motion freeze frame still life portraits of death and dismemberment, and an answer forms in his head.

At some point, the killing has to stop.

Someone has to make the decision to stop it, a unilateral cease fire, one person, one decision at a time.

He glances over his shoulder and sees the cloud bank disappearing behind him, the vast liquid blue of the sea beneath him ahead, the Viper still climbing now out of twenty thousand feet.

Did he press the button, or not?

He cannot be sure, in the state of mind he has been steeped in over the last few moments, of what is and is not real. All he knows is that in his own mind, he made the decision not to. Whether he did so in time, he may never know for sure. He closes his eyes for a moment and sees that girl's face again, her eyes shining silver gray, her lips opened gently, as if to speak.

"So shall they be life unto thy soul, and grace unto thy neck. Then shalt thou walk in thy way safely, and thy foot shall not stumble. When thou liest down, thou shalt not be afraid; yea, thou shalt lie down, and thy sleep shall be sweet."

About the Author

Chris Katsaropoulos is the author of more than a dozen books, including three critically-acclaimed novels, *Fragile, Antiphony* and *Entre-voir,* as well as *Complex Knowing,* the first collection of his poetry. He has been an editor at several major publishing houses and has published numerous trade books, textbooks, and novels over the course of his publishing career. Chris enjoys traveling, playing the piano, and hiking in out of the way places. Visit antiphonyck.blogspot.com to read more, including his most recent poems.